Through The Window

Written by
Michael A. Woodward, Jr.

Illustrated by
Ekaterina Kuznetsova

PUBLISHER'S NOTE

While this is a work of fiction, much of this story is based on true places and events. Names, characters,places, and incidents are the product of the author's imagination or are used fictitiously unless representative of our culture and history.

First paperback and hardcover edition in this format 2020.

Summary: From Africa's Great Rift Valley to the Australian Outback, Michael A. Woodward Jr.'s *ThroughThe Window* takes us on adventures across the world through the imaginative mind of a young scholarwho escapes reality through her bedroom window.

Copyright © Inspire the Masses LLC, 2020. All rights reserved.
Hardcover ISBN: 978-1-0878-7926-0
Paperback ISBN: 979-8-6562-1926-6
Printed in the United States of America
Set in Bembo, with Futura display and Microsoft ornaments.

Written by Michael A. Woodward, Jr.
Cover design and illustrations by Ekaterina Kuznetsova.
Edited by Mallory Miles.

For the dreamers

Through my fifth story window, I see the world and all she has to offer.
I feel her warmth across my cheek, waking me from my slumber.

Sometimes I wake early to snag a front row seat,
V.I.P. access as I know the clouds and the secrets they keep.

There's no need for an alarm. The dogs wake us all,
but you can't be a minute late because through your hands
a golden opportunity may fall.

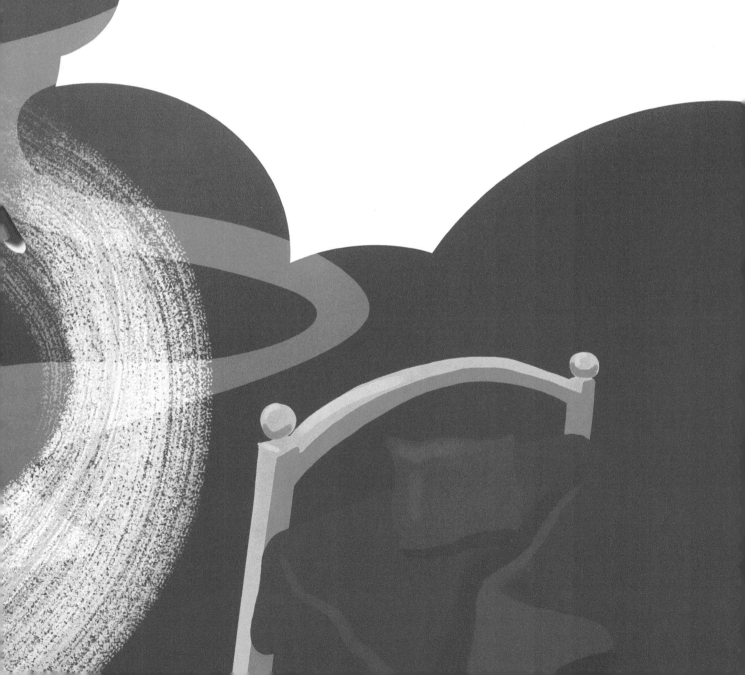

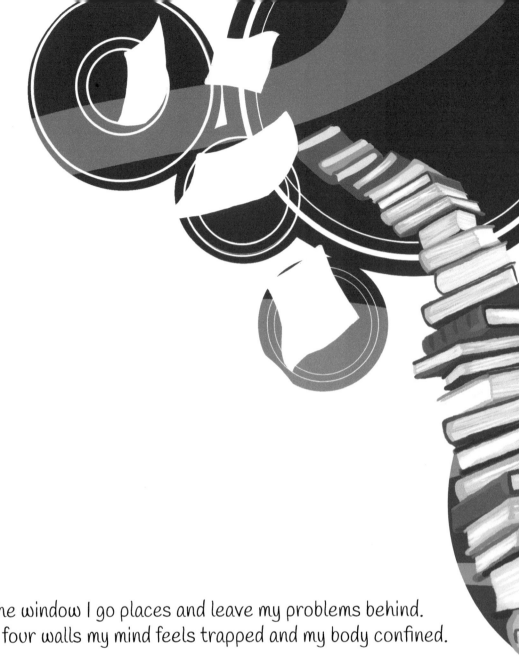

Through the window I go places and leave my problems behind.
Within these four walls my mind feels trapped and my body confined.

It gets stuffy in here; sometimes it's hard to breathe,
so I allow books to take me places and without looking back, I leave.

Oh the places I go and the treasures I carry.
Sometimes leaving the light on because it gets really scary.

I thwart monsters, duel demons, and gouge ghosts in their eyes.
It's like, I open my eyes and I'm there – no lie!

When I look up at the stars, I fix my eyes on the moon.
If I squint hard enough, I can see the wind whisking
through the Saharan sand dunes.

I feel volcanoes shake the room that spew plumes of smoke.
Ashy-black snow blankets the sky forcing the sun to choke.

Bells from a mountain chapel echo with soundwaves of love.
Providing comfort to those who seek shelter from the darkness above.

Then to the jungles of Asia, where I pet a Siberian tiger.
Studying his orange striped camouflage and taking note,
careful not to allow him to claw through my crisp white lab coat.

To the poles tilted furthest,
with eerily caves feeling the coldest.
Dripping with water and lined with bats...
Finding diamonds and rubies buried beneath the rats.

On this bed I lay motionless.
Carried by the tide, sunbaked by the sky,
and drifting alongside a sea of pink anemone.

Ocean winds don't take long to blow down straw dreams of hope.
Meanwhile, the rocking of the boat makes me feel my lunch in my throat.

I take a deep breath to bring myself back to our fifth story apartment.
I kiss my little brother and tell him we were God sent.
He looks back up at me with a glint of hope and an innocent glee.
Being the King I tell him he is, he believes he's royalty.

Sometimes I take him along on the ride and allow him to be free and wander.
We blow bubbles of beliefs to settle our mind's hunger.
But at the next stop I'll tell him he'll have to go, because my imagination flies the furthest when I take my flights solo.

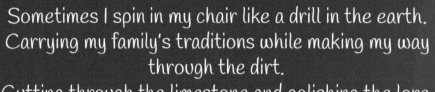

Sometimes I spin in my chair like a drill in the earth.
Carrying my family's traditions while making my way
through the dirt.
Cutting through the limestone and polishing the lore.
Inch by inch, I'll go, until I reach the core.

In the parking lot, I spot a yellow checkered lion with eyes
the color of iron.
Its roar wakes the neighbors as it's towed away by
poachers and slavers.

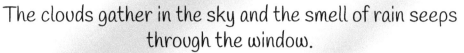

The clouds gather in the sky and the smell of rain seeps
through the window.
Like a shadow, my thoughts trail after me.
Feelings of joy and sounds of glee.
Coupled with mystic waterfalls of wonder is where I'd
rather be.

With a thirst for knowledge dehydrated from pride.
Sometimes on the backs of camels, I'll ride.
Trudging uphill until I find...
A mirage of hope filled with greed and lies.

I hear the pitter-patter of a thousand flamingos shuffling
through Africa's Great Rift Valley.
I see the shadows of masked men waiting patiently for me
to make a wrong turn down the dark alley.

I feel the fur of a koala perched atop my shoulder.
She quivers as The Outback night gets colder.
We grow older.
Swinging from the trees of made-up memories and sun-kissed with the delights of the early Australian Aborigines.

Like a boomerang, I'll come back though...
I'll come back to stare, to dream and glare, to see past the hopelessness of my neighborhood's nightmares.
I know when I dream, away from pain is the direction I'll go.
Because there's always a way out, the more I look through the window.

In the night, I can hear the feet of a forest mouse.
Crunching through dry leaves in hopes the owl is fast asleep.

But the tarantula is wide awake.
She dances in the air, then gets entangled in my hair.
We fight.
Pulling threads of white silk I refuse to lose.
Opening my eyes only to realize...

I'm fighting my stuffed animals once my dad cuts on the light.
He asks me if I'm ok and if I was having a nightmare.
In the silent night, he heard my screams and rescued me with his fatherly care.

I smile and whisper, who sleeps when there are mountains to climb?
With caves to mine and treasures to find?
Daddy, I can't be held back from the true power of my mind.

Inspire The Masses

Michael A. Woodward, Jr. is a former elementary teacher from Miami, FL who earned his bachelor's degree at Florida A&M University (FAMU) and a master's degree from the University of Nevada, Las Vegas (UNLV). Currently, he is working on his doctorate in curriculum and instruction at Barry University.

When Michael isn't typing away on his tablet, you can typically find him somewhere near water in search of a beautiful sunrise, working on his antique muscle car or nestled on the couch with his family watching Jeopardy.

You can visit him at www.michaelwoodwardjr.com

Inspire The Masses

CPSIA information can be obtained
at www.ICGtesting.com
Printed in the USA
LVHW071940050820
662365LV00018B/290

9 781087 879260